The Adventures of Mousie and Lousie

Written by Michael Schildcrout

Illustrated by Ruth Flanigan

PAGE PUBLISHING, INC.
New York, NY

First originally published by Page Publishing, Inc. 2015

ISBN 978-1-63417-083-3 (pbk)
ISBN 978-1-63417-084-0 (digital)

Printed in the United States of America

Contents

Preface

Mouseville is a community of intelligent mice somewhere in the United States. They walk on two feet, wear clothes, and do not have tails. Mousie and Lousie are boy mice fraternal twins. Their cousins, Topsie and Wopsie, are girl mice fraternal twins of about the same age.

Professor Ushgloshkiss Vernes is a somewhat eccentric genius. He has white hair and is somewhere in his fifties. He enjoys working with the intelligent mice from Mouseville. His favorites are Mousie and Lousie.

These stories are dedicated to my younger sister, Alice, to whom I used to tell similar stories using the same set of characters when she was a little girl.

Mousie and Lousie Go on a Picnic with Topsie and Wopsie

It was a fine summer day in Mouseville. The sun was shining, the birds were singing, and there was a nice gentle breeze in the air. Mousie and Lousie decided it was a perfect day to go on a picnic with their cousins, Topsie and Wopsie. So they called up Topsie and Wopsie and arranged to meet them in the city park, which had a big river, lots of trees and grass, and a very nice picnic area. Mousie and Lousie packed a picnic lunch. They packed Swiss cheese and American cheese sandwiches as well as grilled cheese sandwiches. They packed lots of fruits and vegetables, and to drink, they filled a thermos bottle with pink lemonade. They packed it all into a bright green picnic basket. Then they drove to the park in their mousemobile and met Topsie and Wopsie at the picnic area.

It was still early in the day and so nice outside that the four mice thought about leaving their picnic basket in the picnic area while they took a walk in the park along the river. But Topsie was concerned. "What if while we are gone, the ants come along and start eating our food?" Well, Mousie had a good idea to prevent that from happening. "Let's put up a sign saying, 'Ants, please do not eat this food.' That should keep the ants away." The other mice agreed that was a good idea, so they made a sign asking the ants to stay away and placed it on the bright green picnic basket. Now that their picnic food was safe, or so they thought, they could relax and enjoy a nice walk along the river.

Mousie and Lousie, Topsie and Wopsie reached the river and began their walk. They did not get very far when they came across a rowboat along the riverbank. It had two sets of oars for rowing, but the four mice thought it would be even more fun if they could make it into a sailboat and go sailing down the river. So they found some wood, which they fashioned into a frame, and they took an old tablecloth that Mousie just happened to have, and they stretched it across the wooden frame. The tablecloth made an excellent sail, and so off they went sailing down the river.

Mousie and Lousie, Topsie and Wopsie had a good time sailing down the river. The breeze was steady, the water was calm, and they made good progress. They probably would have sailed much farther, but Topsie brought up the question of how were they going to get back up the river. They were already rather far from the picnic area. Well, none of these mice were experienced sailors. But Mousie had a good idea. "Let's remove the sail from the wooden frame, turn the sail around, and then place it back on the wooden frame. That should cause the boat to sail backwards, back up the river." The other mice

agreed that was a good idea. So they removed the sail, turned it around and then placed it back on the wooden frame. But to their surprise, the boat continued sailing down the river just like before. The four mice were beginning to get very hungry and wanted to get back. They finally realized that the only way they were going to get the boat back up the river was to take down the sail and start rowing. So they took down the sail and started rowing the boat up the river to get back to the picnic area.

Mousie and Lousie, Topsie and Wopsie did not get very far rowing the boat up the river when they noticed there was a problem. A small leak had developed at the bottom of the boat. They did not know how to repair the leak, but Mousie had another good idea. The problem, according to Mousie, was that there was only one little hole, so water could only come in the boat. What they needed to do was make another little hole next to the first one so that the water that entered the boat through the first hole could go out the boat through the second hole. The other mice agreed that was a good idea, but when they made the second hole, to their surprise, the water started coming in through both holes. "Well," said Mousie, "it is obvious that since the water is entering through both holes, we need to make two more holes so the water will enter the first two and go out the second two." Soon there were four holes in the bottom of the boat and the water was entering through each one of them. The mice continued making more and more holes until, finally, the boat sank. The four mice had to swim to shore. Now they had no choice but to make the long walk back up the river in their wet clothes. They were cold and hungry, but at least they knew that a wonderful picnic lunch was waiting for them. Or was it?

Meanwhile, back at the picnic area, some ants just happened to come across a bright green picnic basket full of delicious food with a sign saying "Ants, please do not eat this food." Unfortunately, ants cannot read very well. They tried their best, but the only words they could make out were "Ants, please—eat this food." They were so happy that here were picnickers that actually wanted them to help eat the food. The ants were more than happy to help out, so they called up their sisters and brothers and friends and neighbors. Soon there were more than enough ants to help eat all the food.

Finally, after a very long walk, Mousie and Lousie, Topsie and Wopsie arrived at the picnic area. They were tired, hungry, and still wearing their wet clothes. Nevertheless, they were looking forward to a wonderful picnic lunch. But when they reached the bright green picnic basket, to their surprise, in spite of the sign asking the ants to stay away, the basket was now covered with ants. And they were having a big party. They were singing and dancing and munching away at the food. Some of the ants were even wearing party hats. However, for Mousie and Lousie, Topsie and Wopsie, it was an entirely different situation. Their food was spoiled. Their picnic was ruined. It was turning out to be a very bad day.

But Mousie had one last idea.

The four mice got back into Mousie and Lousie's mousemobile and drove back to the house. They went inside and changed into dry clean clothes. They opened a big blanket and spread it on the kitchen floor. They opened the windows to let in fresh air. They opened the refrigerator and took out pizza and French fries, bagels and cream cheese, and cookies and chocolate milk. And then Mousie and Lousie, Topsie and Wopsie had a wonderful picnic right there on the kitchen floor.

Mousie and Lousie Go to the Moon

It was a fine summer day in Mouseville when Mousie and Lousie decided to drive to Washington, DC, the capital of the United States, for a short vacation. There is so much to see in Washington, DC. There is the White House where the president lives; there is the Lincoln Memorial with a big statue of Abraham Lincoln; there is the Washington Monument, a tower made out of white marble; there is the Capitol building with a dome on top that makes it the tallest building in the capital; and much, much more. But Mousie and Lousie were particularly interested in visiting the Smithsonian National Air and Space Museum, one of several museums along the National Mall, a large open area along which visitors could stroll. The Smithsonian National Air and Space Museum specializes in air and space travel.

Mousie and Lousie were particularly interested in finding out about space flight.

So Mousie and Lousie got in their mousemobile and drove from Mouseville to the National Mall in Washington, DC, and from there, they entered the National Air and Space Museum. The two mice joined a group of visitors who were listening to a Smithsonian guide talk about the rocket ships that landed astronauts on the moon six times. The guide also showed the visitors full-scale models of the rocket ships. Mousie and Lousie were very impressed by the exhibit. But Mousie had a question.

"Why build a rocket ship to go to the moon? Why not fly to the moon in an airplane?"

"I know," answered Lousie. "Because there are no gas stations on the way to the moon, so you would run out of gas."

"No," said the guide. "An airplane needs air in order to fly. In outer space, there is no air."

From there, the guide discussed the scientific successes of the moon landings. From each of the six moon landings, the astronauts brought back samples of moon rock and soil. All together, they returned more than eight hundred pounds of material. That prompted Mousie to ask another question.

"I heard there is green cheese on the moon. Did the astronauts bring back any green cheese?"

"No," answered the guide. "That is just a myth. There is no green cheese on the moon."

Mousie was clearly disappointed, but then again the astronauts had not searched every inch of the moon, so maybe there was green cheese on the moon after all, but they just hadn't found it.

That night, back home, the two mice dreamt about the wonders of space travel. Lousie dreamt that they traveled to distant galaxies and met space monsters, friendly ones, of course. They communicated with these strange beings in an intergalactic language that they did not even know they could speak. Meanwhile, Mousie dreamt that they traveled to the moon and found a mountain made of green cheese. The next day, the two mice talked about their dreams of space. They soon realized that the only way to satisfy their curiosity was to travel to space, but where to? Since they were so impressed by the Smithsonian moon landing exhibit, they decided to travel to the moon and see it for themselves.

Mousie and Lousie collected their tools and building materials and traveled to the edge of Mouseville where they were away from the hustle and bustle of the city so they could work in peace and quiet to build their rocket ship to the moon. The landscape at the edge of Mouseville was barren, that is, it lacked trees and grass, just shallow hills and plenty of rocks of all sizes and shapes. Here they worked day and night. Sometimes their cousins, Topsie and Wopsie, stopped by to help out.

Now, building a rocket ship is not easy for people and, certainly, not easy for mice. It requires precision engineering and these mice were not rocket scientists. But finally, their work was complete and the final product sort of resembled a rocket ship.

Finally, the big day arrived when they would go to the moon. Mousie and Lousie carefully aimed the rocket ship toward the moon, got inside, fired up the engines, and took off. The rocket ship slowly lifted off the ground; rose to a height of a few feet, wobbled back and forth; spun around and around; and finally, with a thud, landed in the exact same spot that it started from. Mousie and Lousie were a little shook up and dizzy but otherwise okay

"Wow," said Mousie. "That seemed like a very quick trip to the moon."

"Yes," said Lousie. "We must have been traveling very fast. Now let's go out and explore the moon."

So the two mice put on their space suits along with oxygen tanks, so they could breathe, and walkie-talkie radios, so they could communicate, and stepped outside the spaceship. They were greeted by a barren landscape with plenty of rocks of all sizes and shapes.

"This is awesome," said Mousie.

"Yes," said Lousie. "This is absolutely unbelievable. Here we are on the moon, and the landscape looks so different, like nothing we have ever seen on Earth." The two mice took some time just enjoying the view of the moon landscape. Finally, Lousie said, "We'd better get started collecting moon rocks before we run out of oxygen."

"Yes," replied Mousie. "Moon rocks and green cheese."

So Mousie and Lousie, still wearing their space suits, started walking around collecting rocks of all shapes and sizes and handling them as if they were precious diamonds. Unfortunately, they did not find any green cheese although they did find a broken dish and a rusty spoon. How those items found their way to the moon was a mystery. Finally, when they felt they had collected all the rocks they could carry, they

returned to the spaceship. They carefully aimed the rocket ship toward what they thought was the Earth but sort of looked like the moon. But Mousie was somewhat concerned. "How," asked Mousie "are we going to land near Mouseville? The Earth is very big. We might end up in China."

"I don't know," answered Lousie. "We will just have to try our best. Either that or learn how to speak Chinese."

With that, the two mice got inside the rocket ship with their cargo of rocks, removed their space suits, fired up the engines, and took off. The rocket ship slowly lifted off the ground and rose to a height of a few feet. It wobbled back and forth; spun around and around; and finally, with a real loud thud because of the extra weight of all those rocks, landed in the exact same spot that it started from.

Mousie and Lousie stepped outside the spaceship and examined their surroundings. "Wow," said Mousie. "We must be great navigators. We landed in the same spot on the edge of Mouseville that we started from on our journey to the moon."

"Yes," said Lousie. "What great luck. Now we will not have to learn Chinese after all."

And so when Mousie and Lousie went home that night, they were very satisfied and believed they had a treasure in moon rocks. Later they would find out their rocks were just ordinary earth rocks, but at least for that night, Mousie and Lousie were two very happy mice.

Mousie and Lousie
Return to the Moon

Mousie and Lousie had a cargo of moon rocks, or so they thought, from their trip to the moon. Mousie suggested that they return to the Smithsonian National Air and Space Museum to find out how much their moon rocks were worth. But Lousie had another idea. Instead of traveling all the way back to Washington, DC, why not visit their good friend, Professor Ushgloshkiss Vernes? As a real scientist, he could tell them the same thing. So the two mice invited the good professor to come over to their house and see their collection of moon rocks. Professor Vernes was more than happy to come over and see their collection, but after observing it, he had the strangest feeling that they were ordinary earth rocks. He asked Mousie and Lousie several questions about their trip to the moon. It appeared that although Mousie and Lousie were disoriented by the wobbling and spinning of the rocket ship, so that they could not tell exactly how long the flight took, it was still obvious that the flight time was far too short to actually reach the moon. Next, Professor Vernes asked to see the rocket ship that took Mousie and Lousie to the moon and back. Examining the rocket ship, it was clear it could not have lifted more than a few feet off the ground. So Professor Vernes came to the obvious conclusion that the rocket ship never left Mouseville, and the cargo of rocks were just ordinary earth rocks collected from the outskirts of Mouseville.

Mousie and Lousie were devastated by the news. They so much wanted to believe they had visited the moon, and now they found out not only did they not reach the moon, but also their rock collection, rather than being a treasure, was apparently worthless.

Professor Ushgloshkiss Vernes was very upset to see how disappointed his friends Mousie and Lousie were. In a way, he felt responsible for breaking the bad news and wanted to raise their spirits. So he made up his mind what he would do next. "Mousie and Lousie," said the good professor. "Don't worry. I will build you a rocket ship to take you to the moon." Mousie and Lousie were overjoyed. They could not thank the professor enough. It looked like they were going to the moon after all, so the search for green cheese was back on.

Professor Ushgloshkiss Vernes went to work at his laboratory building a rocket ship for the two mice. After many days of steady work, the rocket ship was complete. It was a bright red rocket ship. Inside there was a control panel with many dials, buttons, and switches. However, the motion of the rocket ship was to be controlled by an onboard computer, so there was really nothing for Mousie and Lousie to do except sit back and enjoy the trip. The inside of the rocket ship also contained a pair of comfortable seats and two beds, since the trip to the moon would take several days. There were also front, back, and side windows so Mousie and Lousie could keep track of their progress approaching the moon. There was a small dining area and, last but not least, a roll of duct tape because duct tape is good for most anything.

Finally, the big day arrived when the professor was to show Mousie and Lousie their rocket ship and they were to take off for the moon. The two mice were delighted with their rocket ship. The professor gave them some last minute instructions, although there wasn't much to tell because the computer would control the rocket ship from takeoff to landing. Mousie and Lousie thanked the professor, got in the rocket ship, and waved good-bye. Mousie hit the start button, and they were off.

Slowly the rocket ship started to rise, and gradually, it picked up speed. Soon they were high up enough to see the entire Earth. What a wonderful sight, a planet filled with color. Around them the sky was dark and filled with stars. Mousie and Lousie were now traveling through space with not much to do except enjoy the scenery. Minutes turned into hours and hours into days. Mousie and Lousie watched the Earth gradually become smaller and the moon gradually become larger.

Now when the rocket ship first took off, Mousie noticed there was a red button on the control panel under which was written "You may or may not want to press this red button." At first, Mousie did not think much about the button, but as time went on and there was not much to do, the red button seemed, at least in his mind, to get bigger and bigger. Mousie could not help wondering what would happen if he pressed the red button. The more he wondered, the harder it became

to resist pressing the red button. After all, there must be some reason that Professor Ushgloshkiss Vernes put it there. So Mousie finally just closed his eyes and pressed the red button.

What they heard next was a recording of Professor Ushgloshkiss Vernes's voice booming over the loudspeaker system. "Mousie and Lousie, you are in for a surprise! My latest hobby has been taking lessons to sing opera, and I will now give you a demonstration of my accomplishments." What followed was the most horrible display of opera singing you can imagine. Professor Ushgloshkiss Vernes had certainly picked the wrong hobby. Lousie joined Mousie in frantically trying to turn off that horrible noise. They tried turning dials, flipping switches and pressing buttons, but still that terrible loud singing continued. And to make matters worse, all that fiddling with dials and switches caused the rocket ship to lose control and start tumbling. After tumbling out of control for what seemed an eternity, Mousie finally noticed a blue button under which was written "If you pressed the red button then you may or may not want to press this blue button." Mousie figured at this point there was nothing to lose, so he pressed the blue button. That terrible singing stopped, and almost immediately, the rocket ship returned to normal. The two mice were very relieved. "Professor Ushgloshkiss Vernes may have good intentions, but he sure is a very strange fellow," said Mousie. "You can say that again," replied Lousie as he used the roll of duct tape to cover up the red button.

Not long afterwards, the display above the instrument panel flashed the warning, "Prepare for landing." The rocket ship slowed down as it began its descent to the moon. Once it landed, Mousie and Lousie put on their space suits along with oxygen tanks, so they could breathe, and walkie-talkie radios, so they could communicate. They exited the rocket ship and took their first steps on the moon. They took time out to enjoy the sight of the lunar landscape and the view of the Earth from the moon. Then they went about collecting the items they planned to bring back with them to Mouseville, moon rocks of all shapes and sizes while keeping an eye out for green cheese.

As Mousie was collecting moon rocks, he came across one that looked quite different than the others. It was round and fuzzy. What a strange rock, thought Mousie. He started picking it up when he distinctly thought he heard it say, "Ouch!" Mousie took a closer look and noticed a pair of eyes.

"Did you say ouch?" asked Mousie.

"Yes," said the fuzzy round rock with eyes.

"You're not a rock," observed Mousie. "So what are you?"

"I am a frataslas," said the round object.

"What is a frataslas?" asked Mousie.

"Well," said the frataslas, "it's a long story, but basically, I like to think of myself as the caretaker or keeper of the moon. Now as keeper of the moon, there is not really that much to do. The moon takes care of itself by doing its own thing like eclipses, half moon, full moon, and so on. So I basically see my job as greeting travelers that land on the moon."

"Have you greeted the Earth astronauts that landed on the moon?" asked Mousie.

"Of course, I did," answered the frataslas.

"Then how come they never mentioned you?" asked Mousie.

"That was the agreement I made with the astronauts as well as all other visitors," answered the frataslas. "I show them my underground living quarters on the condition that they do not reveal that I exist."

"What is wrong about revealing that you exist?" asked Mousie.

"Then they would send their scientists to the moon to find out what kind of life-form I am," answered the frataslas. "They would stick me with pins and needles and do all kinds of tests. I don't want that to happen. So far, all visitors to the moon have kept their word and not revealed my existence."

That prompted Mousie to ask, "Besides the astronauts, who else has visited the moon?"

The frataslas replied, "From time to time visitors from other solar systems stop by the moon."

"Have there been visitors from our solar system besides Earth that have visited the moon?" asked Mousie.

"Yes," said the frataslas. "I have had visitors from the planet Mars, but that was a long time ago."

At that point, Mousie offered to introduce the frataslas to his twin, Lousie. They talked some more, and they learned more about the frataslas. Its way of getting around was to bounce like a ball, so it had no need for feet. It had the ability to move objects with its mind, so it had no need for hands. It had the ability to read thoughts, so Mousie and Lousie could either say words out loud or just think the words. Similarly, it could project its thoughts so that Mousie and Lousie were able to perceive them as words.

The frataslas then offered to take Mousie and Lousie to its underground living quarters under the condition that they would not reveal the frataslas's existence, to which the two mice agreed. The frataslas explained that, a long time ago, there was air and water on the moon; but over time, the air had disappeared and the water had evaporated. The frataslas needed both air and water to live and was forced to go underground where air and water still existed. However, the frataslas also developed the ability to go for long periods of time without air, and that is why Mousie and Lousie were able to find the frataslas on the surface of the moon.

Mousie and Lousie followed the frataslas to a cave in the side of a shallow mountain. They went through a set of doors that served as an air lock to prevent the air in the cave and the rest of the underground dwelling from escaping. Because there was now air, Mousie and Lousie were able to remove their space suits. As the two mice and the frataslas went further into the cave, the dwelling was kept in light by glowing rocks of many colors in the walls and ceiling. Mousie and Lousie and the frataslas followed a path that led to a bridge that crossed an underground river. Continuing their walk, they finally arrived at what is best described as an underground garden. Mousie and Lousie could tell that the garden was growing fruits and vegetables, but they were not able to identify any of them. A little further on, the two mice saw a colorful rug or blanket covering the floor. This was the frataslas's kitchen. Not having hands or feet, the frataslas had no need for a table and chairs.

The frataslas asked Mousie and Lousie to join him for dinner. The two mice realized this was to be sort of a picnic on, or more correctly in, the moon. Through its mind, the frataslas caused fruits and vegetables from the garden to appear in front of Mousie and Lousie. The frataslas then joined them in a wonderful picnic dinner. Each item tasted different than anything either of the mice had ever tasted. The delicious food prompted Mousie to ask the big question.

"Mr. Frataslas, one of the things we came to the moon to search for was green cheese. We were under the impression that there is green cheese on the moon. Is that true?"

"Well," said the frataslas, "I guess the first thing is to search for a fruit or vegetable that is green." Looking through the garden, there was only one plant that had a solid green color. "Come to think of it," said the frataslas, "the astronauts did say this plant had a cheese-like taste."

The frataslas gave some of the green plant to Mousie and Lousie. And would you believe it, it did taste like cheese. Green cheese! Mousie and Lousie thought it was delicious, just as they had always expected green cheese to be. So there really was green cheese on the moon after all. Mousie and Lousie were delighted.

"Can we take some green cheese back with us to Mouseville?" asked Mousie.

"No," said the frataslas. "I'm sorry. Taking back green cheese would give away my existence since I am the one who grows green cheese. But while you are here, have all the green cheese you can eat, and you are always welcome to come back for more."

So Mousie and Lousie and the frataslas enjoyed a wonderful picnic dinner with all kinds of exotic fruits and vegetables and green cheese.

Finally, it was late and time to return to the rocket ship and take off. The frataslas joined Mousie and Lousie on their way back to the rocket ship. The two mice loaded their cargo of moon rocks from the

surface of the moon. They thanked the frataslas for its generosity and prepared to take off. Mousie hit the start button, but the display above the control panel indicated a system overload. Apparently Professor Ushgloshkiss Vernes had miscalculated the amount of fuel they needed to return from the moon. They were forced to leave behind their cargo of moon rocks to reduce weight. Even so, the rocket ship was still too heavy to take off. Mousie and Lousie were not sure what to do next, but the frataslas suggested using its mind power to give the rocket ship an extra boost. And it worked! Soon Mousie and Lousie were on their way back home to Mouseville. They were returning without any items from the moon, but they were satisfied just to have been there and met the frataslas. Now they were privileged to share in a secret that very few were aware —the existence of the frataslas and green cheese on the moon.

A Safari Adventure

The *Mouseville Geographic Magazine* was holding a contest for the best pictures and video of the African lion. First prize was to be a gold-plated trophy depicting the African lion. Mousie, Lousie, Topsie, and Wopsie were interested in entering the contest. But they did not want to pay the expense of hiring a guide or stay at a luxury location. Therefore, they decided to contact Professor Ushgloshkiss Vernes and see if he would be interested in acting as their guide. As a scientist, the professor should know something about just about everything and should therefore make a satisfactory safari guide. Professor Ushgloshkiss Vernes was flattered that the four mice thought so highly of him, and so he agreed to join them on the safari and act as their guide even though he had no safari experience.

To keep expenses to a minimum, the professor chose an African location that had been explored to a minimum. They might find the region packed with wild animals, including the African lion, or it might turn out to be rather barren and empty of wildlife. The professor and the four mice would be living in a rather primitive log cabin with no electricity or hot water, and for transportation for the safari, they were to rent a four-wheel-drive jeep with windows that can be rolled up if they were to face any danger.

Mousie and Lousie, Topsie and Wopsie, and Professor Ushgloshkiss Vernes traveled by airplane from Mouseville to a major city in Africa. From there, they took a small plane to a remote airport. They rented their vehicle at the airport, and with the good professor at the wheel, they drove to their remote lodging, the primitive log cabin. They brought with them cameras and video equipment for still-life photography and for digital movies.

Each day, for several days, Professor Ushgloshkiss Vernes drove while Mousie and Lousie, Topsie and Wopsie rode in the jeep, looking for the African lion, but they came across very little wildlife. They saw squirrels, chipmunks, pigeons, rabbits, turtles, butterflies, but not the kind of wildlife one would expect in Africa. Professor Ushgloshkiss Vernes, Mousie and Lousie, Topsie and Wopsie were getting rather discouraged. Days were going by, and they had nothing to show for it.

Finally they decided that if they could not shoot wildlife pictures and video, particularly that of the African lion, then the least they could do was to have a nice picnic. So they loaded up their jeep with two baskets. A bright green basket held a delicious picnic lunch while another bright green basket held their photography and video equipment. Professor Ushgloshkiss Vernes drove the vehicle to the end of a long, winding dirt road. They took what they thought was the bright green picnic basket out of the vehicle and walked deep into the shrubbery. They found a shady spot underneath a tree ideal for a picnic. They opened the bright green basket and, wait a minute. It was the wrong basket! They accidentally took the bright green basket with the photography and video equipment inside. This would not make a very good picnic lunch. Now someone would have to go back to the jeep to exchange baskets.

But wait another minute! Now out of the bushes came a lion and lioness (lady lion) and the lion and lioness were situated between the five travelers and their jeep. And even worse, the lion and lioness looked very hungry, and it appeared that the good professor and his four friends were on their lunch menu.

Apparently after several days of not finding any significant wildlife, Professor Ushgloshkiss Vernes and his four friends had become careless and done what safari seekers should never do—they left the safety of their vehicle. Now between them and their vehicle was a hungry lion and lioness.

Slowly the lion and lioness approached Professor Ushgloshkiss Vernes and Mousie and Lousie, Topsie and Wopsie. The good professor and four mice knew they could not outrun the lion and lioness. If they did not want to be on the lunch menu, they had to think fast.

So Topsie said to Mousie, "There is an expression, 'Music charms the savage beast.' Didn't you tell me Professor Ushgloshkiss Vernes had taken opera singing lessons?"

"Yes," said Mousie. "But his singing is terrible."

"Have you got a better idea?" asked Topsie.

"No," said Mousie.

"Then let's give it a try," said Topsie.

Lousie and Wopsie also agreed they had no other choice but to give it a try. So the four mice pleaded with the good professor to display his opera singing skills.

Professor Ushgloshkiss Vernes chose as his musical selection a medley of waltzes by Johann Strauss, known as the king of the waltz. To the four mice, his singing sounded terrible as ever, but the wild animals seemed to react differently. At first they looked puzzled, not quite sure what to make of these strange sounds. Then slowly, their expressions turned to recognition and then delight. Then the lion and lioness became partners, and would you believe it, they stood up on their hind legs and began to waltz to the music!

Mousie and Lousie, Topsie and Wopsie could hardly believe what they were seeing. As the lion and lioness waltzed, the four mice quickly removed the video equipment from the bright green basket and started taking pictures and video movies of the lion and lioness waltzing to the singing of the good professor. This went on for quite some time until Professor Ushgloshkiss Vernes motioned that he was running out of musical selections. The good professor and the four mice then began slowly circling around toward the vehicle while the singing continued. Once inside the jeep, they put away the video equipment and drove off in the safety of their vehicle. Looking back, the lion and lioness were still dancing, apparently to the music still playing in their heads.

Professor Ushgloshkiss Vernes, Mousie and Lousie, Topsie and

Wopsie finally had what they had traveled to Africa for—a one-of-a-kind video of the African lion. The next day, they packed up their belongings, left Africa, and returned to Mouseville. They entered their pictures and video of the dancing lions in the Mouseville Geographic Magazine's contest. Their pictures and video easily won first prize. Each of them—Professor Ushgloshkiss Vernes, Mousie and Lousie, Topsie and Wopsie—received a gold-plated trophy depicting the African lion. And Professor Ushgloshkiss Vernes, in his own way, had truly proven his worth as a safari guide.

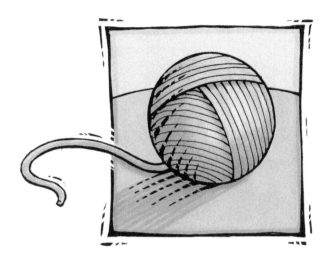

The Start of the Mousie and Lousie Detective Agency

When Mousie and Lousie started their detective agency, it was several weeks before they got their first call. Finally, a Mrs. Jones called saying her cat, Buster, was up in a tree and couldn't get down. Mousie asked, "Why not call the fire department? Detective agencies do not remove cats from trees." Mrs. Jones explained she had called the fire department several times before to get Buster down from the tree, and now they were telling her they had more important things to do. Since Mousie and Lousie had no other business, they decided Mousie would go over to get Buster down.

When Mousie arrived at Mrs. Jones's house, she showed Mousie the tree and Buster high up in the top branches. Buster was a twenty-seven-pound cat that loved to climb this particular tree, but kept

forgetting how to get down. Mousie assured Mrs. Jones that he would get Buster down, though, the fact is, he didn't know how, short of cutting down the tree. Reassured, Mrs. Jones went back into the house.

Mousie did not have a ladder to reach the cat, so he thought of another way to get Buster down. Mousie ran around the tree, making funny faces at Buster, figuring the cat would eventually become so annoyed as to find its own way down. After half an hour of such antics, Buster became sufficiently annoyed that he did find his way down as Mousie had hoped. Once down, Buster chased Mousie around the tree until Mousie finally climbed the tree to get away from Buster. Now Mousie was wondering how he was going to get down from the tree as Buster sat there waiting for him.

Luckily for Mousie, Mrs. Jones opened the front door and, seeing Buster down from the tree, called him inside the house. A very relieved Mousie then climbed down the tree. Mousie was then able to go inside the house to collect his fee. Mrs. Jones asked Mousie what he was doing up in the tree after Buster had already come down. Mousie was embarrassed to give the real reason, so he said he was inspecting the branches to make sure they were sturdy.

And so ended the first case of the Mousie and Lousie Detective Agency. It certainly was not much of a detective case, but at least it was a start.

The Case of
the Missing Cake

It was a dark and stormy night when a call came in to the Mousie and Lousie Detective Agency. It came from a Mrs. Smith requesting help to solve a mystery. Mousie and Lousie arrived at the given address and were greeted at the door by Mr. and Mrs. Smith. Inside, their son Howard was having a birthday party with seven of his friends. Mrs. Smith invited Mousie and Lousie to come inside and said she would explain what happened.

Inside the house, the eight children were seated at a round table. Sandy, the Smith's golden retriever, was settled down on the rug. The Smiths other pet Rusty, a petite short-haired cat, was lying under the sofa and wearing a set of booties that looked a little too large on her.

Mrs. Smith then explained the mystery: She brought in the birthday cake, a layer cake with vanilla frosting, and the children sang happy birthday to Howard. Howard blew out the candles on the birthday cake, and then Mrs. Smith divided the cake into eight equal pieces and gave a piece to each child. No sooner had she distributed the cake than there was a lightning strike that knocked out the electricity, leaving everyone in the dark. Mr. Smith asked the children to stay seated and not move while he went to the basement to reset the circuit breakers. The house was in the dark for about three minutes. When the lights came back on, the cake was missing from Howard's plate. Each of the children denied eating Howard's cake. Mrs. Smith wanted Mousie and Lousie to find out what happened to the missing cake.

Mousie suggested that maybe the culprit did not eat the cake but merely hid it. He proposed that they turn off the lights again for another three minutes to give the culprit a chance to return the cake without a penalty. Mr. and Mrs. Smith agreed, so they turned off the lights for another three minutes. When the lights were turned back on, a second piece of cake belonging to another child was missing. The culprit had struck again.

Mousie asked to examine the two empty plates to see if they could provide any clues. Mousie took out his magnifying glass to examine the two plates. What he saw seemed to solve the mystery. Both plates had paw prints on them, and the paw prints matched those of Sandy, the golden retriever. Apparently when the lights were out, Sandy must have jumped onto the table and eaten the cake. So the children were telling the truth when they denied eating the cake. The real culprit was the golden retriever, Sandy. And so the case of the missing cake seemed to be solved.

But to Lousie, something did not seem right. For one thing, Sandy

did not appear to look guilty when Mrs. Smith scolded her for eating the cake. The second thing, how could a sixty-five-pound dog like Sandy jump on to the table without anyone noticing? Lousie then asked about the booties that Rusty the cat was wearing. They seemed a little too big on her. Mrs. Smith explained that she made the booties for Sandy when Sandy was a puppy. When Sandy outgrew the booties, Mrs. Smith turned them over to Rusty. Rusty, being a clever cat, learned how to take them off and put them on by herself. She usually did not wear the booties, but tonight, for some reason, she wanted to wear them.

Lousie asked if he could examine the booties. Mrs. Smith agreed, and Rusty reluctantly let Mrs. Smith remove her booties so Lousie could examine them. Lousie noticed that the impression of golden retriever paw prints was sewn on the bottom of each booty. When Lousie asked about that, Mrs. Smith replied that she had forgotten that when she made the booties, she sewed paw prints on the bottom of each booty to make the booties unique for Sandy. Lousie also noticed that pieces of vanilla frosting were also visible on the bottom of the booties along with the paw prints.

Lousie concluded that it was Rusty the cat, wearing her booties (with golden retriever paw prints sewn at the bottom), who was the real culprit. She was the one who had jumped on the table when the lights went out and had eaten the cake. Mousie agreed, and so did Mr. and Mrs. Smith. So the Mousie and Lousie Detective Agency successfully solved the case of the missing cake.

Mrs. Smith then cooked a delicious cherry pie and made sure there was more than enough for everyone, including the pets and Mousie and Lousie. And this time, the lights did not go out.

The Case of the Missing Lawn Ornaments

One early morning, the Mousie and Lousie Detective Agency received a call from Mr. Clay. Mr. Clay was the president of a neighborhood watch committee, and lately, several residents had reported missing lawn ornaments and other assorted items they left outside. Mr. Clay wanted Mousie and Lousie to come over to his residence early because, by midmorning, he had to be at his day job. (Members of neighborhood watch committees do this on a voluntary basis, so most of them have to go to work at their regular jobs just like anyone else.)

Mousie and Lousie jumped in their Mousemobile and arrived at Mr. Clay's house at 6:00 a.m. Mr. Clay explained that none of the missing items were expensive, but replacing them was still a nuisance, so they wanted to catch whoever was doing this. Mousie noticed that in Mr. Clay's backyard was a very big doghouse, for a very big dog. Mr. Clay said the dog's name was Rocky, and she was a big black Rottweiler. She was very gentle, so Mousie and Lousie spent a little time playing with her. Afterwards, Mr. Clay showed Mousie and Lousie the locations that neighborhood watch personnel had used to watch, without success, for the culprit that was taking the lawn ornaments.

Mr. Clay said that it seemed like the lawn ornaments disappeared between two and four o'clock in the morning. The items that disappeared were statues of pink flamingoes, gnomes of various sizes and shapes, an umbrella, a pogo stick, and a couple of baseballs (but not the baseball gloves or bats). Nothing taken was of much value, which led Mr. Clay to suspect the culprit was a prankster who was not after valuables but just trying to be a nuisance. Either that or he or she was a thief with very bad taste.

Once back at their detective agency, they discussed the case. Lousie noted that Rocky, Mr. Clay's Rottweiler, had a slightly damp coat, as if she had been out in the rain the night before. It had rained the previous night between two and four o'clock in the morning, the same time that the lawn ornaments seemed to have disappeared. Mousie noted that none of the lookout points that Mr. Clay had shown them had a clear view of his property. Mousie and Lousie began to suspect that the culprit might not be a person but a very friendly big dog named Rocky.

The following night, at close to two o'clock in the morning, Mousie and Lousie drove their mousemobile to a location that had a clear view of Mr. Clay's backyard. Mousie was at the steering wheel while Lousie was ready to work a camera attached to the dashboard. At exactly 2:15 a.m., Rocky emerged from her dog house, left the backyard, and began

roaming the neighborhood. Mousie started the mousemobile to follow her, and Lousie turned on the camera. Rocky roamed for about a mile, passing by several houses. Finally she found what she was looking for, another pink flamingo lawn ornament. She grabbed it with her mouth and went trotting back home. Once at home, she put the pink flamingo in her large doghouse, came out, yawned, went back in, and presumably went to sleep. The time was 3:35 a.m. Mousie asked Lousie if he got it all on camera, which Lousie confirmed. So Mousie and Lousie, their mission complete, drove back home.

Early the next day, Mousie called Mr. Clay and asked if they could come over. Mr. Clay agreed, so by 6:00 a.m., Mousie and Lousie arrived at Mr. Clay's house. They showed him the video taken the night before. Mr. Clay was dumbfounded. He never suspected his beloved dog Rocky to be the culprit. Mr. Clay went into his backyard and looked into the doghouse. There beside a happy Rocky were nine statues of pink flamingoes, gnomes of various sizes and shapes, an umbrella, a pogo stick, a couple of baseballs, and some assorted pieces of junk.

So Mr. Clay was left with the embarrassing task of letting the neighborhood know that he, the president of the neighborhood watch committee, was responsible for the missing items. Of course, he could not blame Rocky. This gentle dog had no idea she was doing anything wrong. Mr. Clay would have to find some way of changing Rocky's behavior. In any case, thanks to Mousie and Lousie, the missing items could now be returned to their rightful owners, and another mystery was solved.

Mousie Fights for the Heavyweight Championship of the World

In just a few more months, Helios Weed would begin his tenth year as boxing's heavyweight champion of the world. He had already beaten all top contenders, but he still wanted to remind the world what a great champion he was. So he was discussing with his staff the idea of a tenth anniversary championship fight. Unlike his other fights, the contender would be picked at random from a pool of submitted names in which anyone could enter. While no one really expected a contender picked in such a manner to have much of a chance of beating the heavyweight champion, the fight was to be more of an entertainment event than a boxing match. Helios would enter the ring among lots of showmanship, and people would marvel how generous he was to give the average person a chance to win the heavyweight championship of the world. Most of those entering the pool were professional or semiprofessional boxers. But Lousie, as a joke, submitted Mousie's name, knowing the chance of it being selected was near zero. And so Helios Weed selected a name entirely at random from the pool, and that lucky name turned out to be Mousie's.

When Mousie heard that he had been selected, he was angry at Lousie for entering his name and was ready to turn down the offer. He knew he had no chance of winning, but Lousie reminded him that the money paid well, so in the end, Mousie reluctantly accepted.

Mousie asked Lousie to be his manager and Topsie and Wopsie to be his seconds. They chose a local gym where Mousie could begin training. Things did not go well at the gym. Mousie had lots of trouble with the punching bag. Often on the rebound, it would knock him down and occasionally knock him out. Also, finding a sparring partner was a problem because they were all far better boxers than he was. In the end, the owner of the gym told Mousie that he had no talent for boxing and asked him to leave.

Mousie realized that in the boxing match with Helios Weed he would have to rely on the one thing he was good at, and that was running. Also, at Lousie's suggestion, he held meetings with the good Professor Ushgloshkiss Vernes for a secret strategy that might help him in the fight.

Every morning at five o'clock, Mousie began his running routine, running through the streets of Mouseville. Those Mouseville residents awake at that hour thought he was running to build up stamina for the fight. Actually, Mousie was running just for the sake of running, so he could run faster in the ring.

Finally came the weigh-in the day before the fight. Helios Weed weighed in at a trim 215 pounds. Mousie weighed in at, well, they didn't know because his weight was too low to register on the scale.

And then came the night of the fight. Helios Weed made his way from the locker room to the ring, sitting on a king's throne hoisted by four strong men and with a golden crown on his head. Surrounding the throne and the four men hoisting it were a bunch of dancing ladies. All the while the loudspeakers were playing loud dance music. The procession slowly made its way from the locker room to the ring. Helios Weed wanted to make sure the crowd had plenty of time to take notice of the world champion.

Next to enter the ring was Mousie, followed by his manager, Lousie, and the seconds, Topsie and Wopsie. There were no dancing ladies or loud dance music for Mousie. In fact, most people did not even notice Mousie enter the ring

Soon it was time for the ring announcer to introduce the fighters. "Ladies and gentlemen, can I have your attention? In this corner, weighing 215 pounds and with an excellent record of thirty-six wins, no defeats, and thirty-three wins by knockout, and tonight, celebrating his tenth year as heavy weight champion of the world, Helios Weed!" This brought a big cheer from the crowd. "And in this corner fighting for the first time and weighing less than our heavyweight scale registers, from Mouseville, USA, Mousie!" There was dead silence.

Then after the referee gave final instructions to both boxers, the bell rang, starting the first round. Mousie immediately began running away from Helios, and Helios began chasing him. Mousie's morning runs seemed to pay off as he managed to stay a step or two ahead of Helios. The crowd began to boo, but Mousie did not let up. His

strategy, at this point, was to survive anyway he could, and that meant running away from his opponent. Sometimes he ran clockwise, other times counter clockwise, sometimes in a crossing pattern, but he always remained a step or two ahead of Helios Weed. Once he even tried hiding behind the referee, but the boos became so loud that he gave up on that strategy. So the first round ended with neither fighter landing a punch.

The second round was no different than the first except the boos were a bit louder as Mousie continued to run and Helios continued to chase him. The same went with round three. At one point, Helios yelled at Mousie in frustration "Stand still and fight! What are you, a man or a mouse?"

"I'm a mouse," cried Mousie as he continued to run.

The fourth and fifth rounds were more of the same. Mousie continued to run from Helios, and the crowd continued to boo. The referee was thinking of stopping the fight and disqualifying Mousie, but the crowd was already in such a bad mood that the referee was afraid a stoppage would cause a riot, so the referee let the fight (if that's what you want to call it) continue.

In the sixth round, Mousie was still running away from Helios when Mousie tripped on his shoelace. This allowed Helios to finally catch up to Mousie. Helios threw a right uppercut. This caught Mousie square on the chin and knocked him up and out of the ring. Luckily, Mousie landed on Topsie and Wopsie, who immediately administered smelling salts and shoved him back in the ring. Mousie beat the count and continued to run for the rest of the round.

Rounds 7 through 11 were more of the same. Mousie ran while Helios chased him. The only difference was Helios was noticeably getting tired. He had trained to fight, not to run. Still, as the aggressor, Helios was winning every round, even without throwing a punch.

At the end of round 11, Lousie reminded Mousie that they were going into the twelfth and final round. Now Mousie had to use the strategy he worked on with Professor Ushgloshkiss Vernes.

The bell rang for round 12. From the beginning of the round, Mousie kept running away from Helios. Helios was tired and was chasing him more slowly. Finally, Mousie built up enough of a lead to allow himself to climb up on to the top rope in a neutral corner, still facing the ring, before Helios caught up to him. Helios was completely confused as to why Mousie was suddenly making himself such an easy target. He was so confused that he didn't know what to do. Then Mousie said to Helios, "Look me in the eyes." When Helios did, Mousie continued in a calm voice, "Your eyelids are getting heavy. You are very tired. You want to close your eyes and go to sleep."

Yes, the secret strategy Mousie had worked on with Professor Ushgloshkiss Vernes was hypnosis. Hypnosis works best when the subject is tired, and Helios was very tired after chasing Mousie for eleven rounds. Before long, Helios was in a hypnotic trance. Then Mousie punched him in the nose. Helios wobbled back and forth, back and forth, back, and finally, with a loud thud, landed flat on his back on the canvas while still in a trance.

The crowd was dead silent as the referee began to count, "One, two, three"—now they were beginning to cheer—"four, five, six"—now they were cheering louder, realizing that in just four more counts, there will be a new world champion—"seven"—louder—"eight"—louder and louder—"nine"—loudest! Now the referee could hardly hear himself count. In just one more count, Mousie will be the new world champion. And just as the referee was about to count ten, *bong bong bong*! The bell rang. The fight was over. Helios Weed was saved by the bell.

The referee read the decision by the judges at ringside. As expected, all scorecards had it eleven rounds to one in favor of the champion in this rather strange fight in which only two punches were thrown. However this time, when Mousie and company left the ring, people took notice, and Mousie and Lousie, Topsie and Wopsie received a good round of applause.

The next day, Helios' manager called Mousie on the phone and offered a rematch. Apparently Helios Weed was embarrassed that he almost lost the heavyweight championship of the world to a mouse. However, Mousie made it clear that he was through with boxing. He knew he did not have real boxing talent. Once was enough, and he was perfectly satisfied with the outcome of his one and only boxing match.

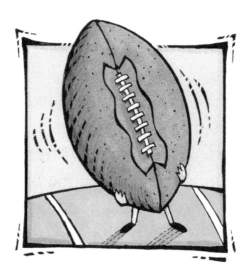

Mousie and Lousie
Play Football

The town of Mouseville is located in a county called Orange County. There are several other towns and small cities located in Orange County besides Mouseville, so the vast majority of residents in Orange County are people, not mice. Surrounding Orange County are a number of other counties, each of which has the name of a color. So for example, there is Green County, Yellow County, Red County, Blue County, and so on. Each of these counties, including Orange County, has a countywide football team, and these teams play each other every year during the football season. At the end of the football season, the two best teams play for the championship of the color counties.

One day, Topsie and Wopsie came over to visit Mousie and Lousie. They found them in their backyard playing with a football. Topsie and Wopsie wanted to know what this was all about because mice do not normally play football. Mousie and Lousie explained that they planned to try out for the Orange County football team. Of course, as mice, they could not do all the things that people do, such as block, tackle, throw or catch passes, and so on. After all, a football is bigger than they are, but they found there was one thing they could do, and that was run fast with the football. When they run, they wear special sticky gloves and hold the ball in both hands down at the point so that the ball is in a vertical, upright position. This presents the problem that the ball is held in front of the face, reducing vision. "But that is just something we'll have to get used to," said Mousie. So Topsie and Wopsie wished Mousie and Lousie good luck and let them continue with their practice.

The next day, Mousie and Lousie paid a visit to the coach of the orange team and expressed their desire to join the team. They showed the coach how they could run with the football. The coach was impressed with their running ability, but because of their other limitations compared to people, they could not be starters. The coach said he would use them in football games as special opportunities came up.

So Mousie and Lousie became members of the orange team. It took a while, but finally, football uniforms were tailored to their size. Mousie and Lousie showed up early each week before game time but spent the entire game sitting on the bench in their football uniforms. It was as if the coach forgot all about them. Nevertheless, their team did well and ended the regular season in a tie with the green team for first place, so the championship game was going to pit the green team against the orange team.

Now we are at the championship game between the green and orange teams. It is a game between two evenly matched teams, and the score keeps fluctuating back and forth. It looks like there is a very good chance that the outcome will be decided by the final few plays of the game. As it turns out, it is the final play of the game that will determine the outcome. The green team is winning by four points, 45–41. The orange team has the ball on the green team's thirty-yard line. It is fourth down, and the orange team has called its last time out with three seconds left in the game. They need a touchdown because a field goal only adds three points. Everyone expects the orange team to go with one final Hail Mary pass to the end zone. That is, everyone except the coach of the orange team. Instead, he finally calls in Mousie and Lousie. The quarterback is to hand off to Mousie, and he is to run for the touchdown. Lousie is to back him up. The advantage of using Mousie and Lousie is the green team has never seen them run.

So the orange team quarterback, instead of fading back to throw a Hail Mary pass, hands the ball off to Mousie. Mousie is initially confused because the football is blocking his view. He quickly recovers and is off running for a touchdown. Mousie has a clear field ahead of him. All he has to do is keep running. The crowd is cheering him on. None of the other players are able to catch up to him. Some are shouting something, but Mousie cannot make out what they are shouting due to the crowd noise. Probably they are just frustrated that they cannot catch him. The cheering drives him on. He runs with his head up and his chest out. This has to be one of his finest moments, and he wishes it could last forever.

But, suddenly, something seems wrong. It was thirty yards for a touchdown, but Mousie seems to have run more than thirty yards

and is not in the end zone yet. Also, the orange team cheering section should be on his left, but the cheering is coming from the right. Now Mousie can make out what some of the players are yelling. "You're running the wrong way!" Mousie can now see the wrong end zone right in front of him. In order not to go over it, he slams on his brakes. He skids to the goal line, loses his balance, and wobbles backwards and forward, backwards and, oh no! He falls forward over the goal line and into the end zone, giving the other team a touchdown. The green team players are jumping up and down, thinking they have won the game.

But wait a minute. Mousie dropped the ball before he fell over the goal line. The ball is in front of the goal line and still in play. And wait another minute! Here comes Lousie to scoop up the football and start running with it. And he is running in the right direction. In the meantime, most of the green team players are still celebrating, thinking they have won the game. Others see a football seemingly moving on its own and don't know what to make of it. Lousie has a clear field ahead of him and takes advantage of it. Now it is the orange team section that is cheering. Lousie has one last green team player to beat. This player is standing in front of the goal line with his legs apart, so he can more easily go left or right. Lousie simply runs straight through his legs and makes the touchdown. The game is over. The orange team has won. Regarding Mousie and Lousie, the coach doesn't know whether to box their ears or congratulate them.

In any case, it is the end of the football season. There are winners and losers, but they all get another chance next year. Mousie and Lousie just happen to be among this year's winners.

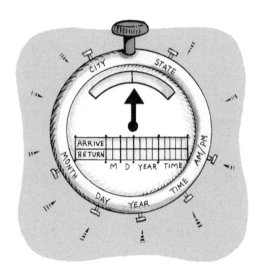

Mousie and Lousie
Go Back in Time: One Day

One day, Mousie and Lousie decided to visit Professor Ushglosh-kiss Vernes and see what he was up to. They found the good professor busy at work in his laboratory, working on a device that looked like a pocket watch. (A pocket watch is similar to a wristwatch except it is larger and has no strap to keep it on your wrist. Instead you keep it in your pocket. It usually has a chain that can be attached to a belt loop to keep it from getting lost. Old time train conductors and bus drivers used to use pocket watches.)

Mousie asked the good professor what he was doing with a pocket watch. Professor Vernes explained that it was more than a pocket watch. It was a time machine. He hoped that one day it would allow people to go back anywhere in time, but for now, its limit was one

day. "After all," he said, "the Wright brothers, when they invented the airplane, did not start off with a jet plane that could go faster than the speed of sound. They started with a strange looking contraption that flew for only twelve seconds on its first flight." Similarly, this was the professors first attempt at a time machine, and he wanted to start off slow to make sure he had the basics correct.

Mousie asked, "What good is a time machine that only goes back in time one day?" Professor Vernes replied that it was good enough to test his theory that you cannot, by going back in time, substantially change the future. Perhaps you can make small changes, but nothing that will have a lasting effect into the future. He said he would like Mouse and Lousie to test his theory by going back one day in time and using their knowledge of the next day to see if they could change their fortune for the better.

Mousie said he knew just what to do. He noticed that in yesterday's results at the racetrack, a horse that was a ten-to-one underdog won the race. That meant if he had bet one hundred dollars on this horse, he would have won ten times a hundred, or a thousand dollars. Mousie asked Professor Vernes if he considered that a substantial change in fortune. The good professor agreed, saying "With the one thousand dollars you could, for example, go to Europe and have a very nice vacation with all kinds of new adventures that otherwise may not be possible." Professor Vernes said he believed that since winning a thousand dollars was a lasting change to the future, that if Mousie and Lousie went back a day in time and tried to win a thousand dollars, they would fail. Mousie and Lousie disagreed. So the professor said the only way to find out was to try it.

Mousie and Lousie agreed to give it a try, so Professor Vernes gave both Mousie and Lousie a time machine pocket watch. He showed them how to set the dials for going back in time and for returning to the present. Once these times are set, you press a red button, which locks in the information and starts the time machine. So Mousie and Lousie set their pocket watch time machines identically for going back and returning, pressed the red buttons, and a moment later they were back in time to the previous day.

When Mousie and Lousie went back one day in time, the first thing that happened was they met the Mousie and Lousie from the day before at their house. It was as if Mousie had an identical twin and Lousie also had an identical twin, except Time-machine Mousie and Time-machine Lousie were one day older than their identical twins. Time-machine Mousie and Lousie had a lot of explaining to do to their identical twin Mousie and Lousie from the previous day. They told them about the time machine and their experiment to see if they could change their future for the better by using their new knowledge to win a thousand dollars at the horse races. After some further discussions about the time machines, the two sets of Mousies and Lousies decided it was best to break up in order to avoid confusing Mouseville residents who might be wondering why there were two sets of Mousies and Lousies. So Mousie and Lousie from the previous day went over to visit Topsie and Wopsie, while Time-machine Mousie and Lousie went to the racetrack to win a thousand dollars.

We will now follow Time-machine Mousie and Lousie at the racetrack. For simplicity, we will just call them Mousie and Lousie. At the racetrack, there were several horse races. Mousie knew that the winning horse for the third race was the ten-to-one underdog. Unfortunately he forgot the horse's name, but he remembered it consisted of

two words and had something to do with the weather. So when Mousie saw that for the third race there was a ten-to-one underdog called Windy Weather, he knew that must be the one. So Mousie went to the cashier booth and bet one hundred dollars on Windy Weather.

As the race started, Windy Weather was in last place. One-fourth through the race, Windy Weather was still in last place. Halfway through the race, Windy Weather had not changed from last place. Mousie was getting worried. Maybe this horse makes a run for it late in the race. But three quarters through the race, Windy Weather was still in last place. Now they were on the final stretch of the race. If Windy Weather was going to move up and win, it was now or never. It turned out to be never. When the race was over, Windy Weather came in last. The winning horse was April Showers, also a ten-to-one underdog. So Mousie had bet on the wrong weather horse. Now, not only did he not win a thousand dollars, he lost the one hundred dollars that he had bet. He would have been better off not to have bet at all.

In the meantime while the race was going on, Lousie, who was not interested in horse racing, stopped by the gambling casino that was on the racetrack grounds. Lousie had nothing but a single quarter in his pocket and figured he might just as well use it on one of the slot machines. (These machines have a lever. You drop your coin in a slot, pull the lever, and if the display shows three of a kind, then you are a winner.) Well, when Lousie pulled the lever, a siren went off, and lights started flashing. Lousie thought he must have done something terribly wrong and was about to get arrested. But then quarters started pouring out of the machine. Lousie then realized he had hit the jackpot, which is a very rare event. Lousie started collecting all the quarters he could by stuffing them in his pockets. Soon his pockets were overflowing with quarters, and they were still flowing out of the machine. Someone kindly gave him a canvas bag for collecting the rest of the quarters. In total, Lousie collected four hundred quarters for a total of one hundred dollars.

Later on, when Mousie and Lousie met up, they talked about their earnings at the racetrack. All in all, they came out even. They won as much money as they lost. So at least in this case, it appeared that the good professor was correct: going back to the past did not enable Mousie and Lousie to make lasting changes to the future. They did not win the thousand dollars they were so sure about. And so, when time was up and Mousie and Lousie returned with their time machines back to the present, it was as if nothing had ever happened.

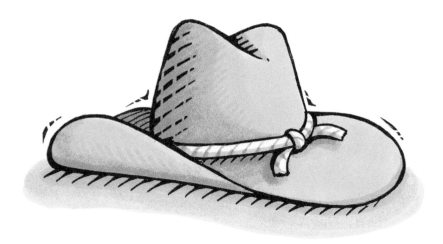

Mousie and Lousie Go Back in Time: The Wild West

Several weeks had passed since Mousie and Lousie had tested Professor Ushgloshkiss Vernes's time machine for going back one day in time. Now the good professor gave them a call to tell them that the time machine could go back further in time, probably to the 1870s. Far enough to allow Mousie and Lousie to go back in time to the Wild West. Mousie and Lousie were delighted to hear the news that they could go back to the Wild West and dress as cowboys. They dropped what they were doing and immediately went over to see Professor Vernes.

The professor showed them the time machines, which were basically the same as the ones they used before, except now they needed to enter a bit more information. In addition to setting the times for going into the past and returning to the present, they now had to specify a location to go to. Other than that, it was the same. The good professor gave a pocket watch time machine to Mousie and another pocket watch time machine to Lousie. They arbitrarily set the start date as 11:00 a.m., May 7, 1875, and the return date as 8:00 p.m. the same day. As for location, they set it for Silver City in southern New Mexico. Mousie and Lousie made sure their time machine pocket watches were identically set, pressed the red buttons, and just like that, they were back in time.

The first thing Mousie and Lousie had to do was buy cowboy clothes so they would fit in with the rest of the town. They brought along a bunch of silver dollars dated in the eighteen hundreds, so money was no concern. They each bought a gun and holster, and of course, cowboy hats and cowboy boots. Now they were ready to stop by the local saloon.

So, in through the swinging gates of the saloon came Mousie and Lousie. No one paid them much attention. That was just as well. They were content to just look around. Some people were playing poker; others were drinking beer and having a lively discussion. There were even a few people listening to the piano player.

Lousie wanted to go to the bar and order a drink. He had never been in a bar before, so he asked Mousie what he should ask for. Mousie said "Ask for your favorite drink." So Lousie called over the bar tender and said, "I'll have a glass of chocolate milk." The bartender asked sarcastically, "Will that be with two teaspoons of chocolate syrup or three?" Ignoring the sarcasm, Lousie said "With three please." Then the young man sitting next to him asked if he would like it in a baby bottle or would a glass be okay. Lousie found that one hard to ignore.

So he said to the young man, "You better watch your step and what you say. My friend here happens to be the fastest gun in town, and he doesn't appreciate that kind of talk." Now Mousie did not want to contradict his twin brother Lousie, but he had never used a gun before, so he didn't know what to do. As a result, he didn't do anything. Now the young man said to Lousie, "Your friend says he is the fastest gun in town, and I say I'm the fastest gun in town, so what should we do?"

Mousie tried to cool things down by saying, "Let's forget the whole thing. By the way, my name is Mousie. What's yours?"

"William McCarty," said the young man.

Mousie almost froze. He recognized William McCarty as the name of the outlaw later referred to as Billy the Kid.

Then McCarty said, "I think we need to settle this thing about who is the fastest gun in town. Meet me here at six o'clock, and we will have a draw for the fastest gun in town."

Mousie knew he had no chance against the future Billy the Kid, so knowing he was due back to the present at 8:00 p.m., he said. "If you don't mind, I'd like to enjoy my supper. I eat kind of slowly, so how about we meet here after supper at 8:05 p.m.?"

"No," said McCarty. "Six o'clock it is. Be here." And with that he left the saloon.

Mousie could have strangled Lousie for getting him into this predicament. Lousie tried to defend himself by replying, "How was I to know he's the future Billy the Kid. He looked like some weakling teenager, and I thought I could scare him by telling him you are the fastest gun in town." Mousie realized there was no point arguing. Now the question was how to get ready to draw against Billy the Kid.

So Mousie and Lousie found an empty lot with a broken-down fence. They put some rocks on top of the fence, and Mousie tried to draw and shoot the rocks. After several attempts, the fence was full of holes and all the rocks were still in place. Mousie realized no matter how much he practiced he could never be as accurate as McCarty. He figured all he could do was give it his best effort and hope for a miracle.

And so the hours slowly went by as six o'clock approached. Finally, the town bell rang six times, indicating it was six o'clock. Then out of the saloon came McCarty, looking so calm you would think it was a typical spring day. Meanwhile, Mousie was doing his best to keep from shaking. McCarty stood in front of the saloon while Mousie was on the other side of the street. Unknown to Mousie, McCarty had seen him practicing and realized Mousie could not hit the side of a barn from ten feet away. There was no glory in shooting a mouse who could not shoot straight, so McCarty planned to let Mousie take the first shot. He would miss, of course. Then McCarty would shoot a hole in Mousie's hat and leave it at that.

Now McCarty and Mousie faced each other. Mousie could not help shaking from fear. On the other hand, McCarty was perfectly calm. Finally, Mousie drew his gun and fired. The bullet hit a water bucket, ricocheted off the metal rim, hit the brick wall of the saloon, ricocheted off the wall, and hit the support for the saloon sign. As a result, the sign fell down, hitting McCarty square on the head, knocking him out.

Lousie looked over at Mousie and saw him lying on the ground. He went over and asked "Mousie, what's wrong?" Mousie said, "Get the doctor. I have been shot." Lousie said, "No, you haven't. He never

fired his gun." Mousie felt around. Sure enough, he was okay. A very relieved Mousie sprang to his feet. The crowd applauded to see that Mousie was not hurt.

In the meantime, the doctor was called to examine McCarty. The prognosis here was that McCarty would probably be out for another two or three hours. He had a big bump on his head from getting hit by the falling saloon sign, but he was going to fully recover.

There was a controversy among people in the crowd. Some said Mousie couldn't shoot straight, and his shot was pure luck. Others insisted he was a trick shooter and the crooked shot was intentional. Some said he outdrew McCarty. Others said McCarty let him shoot first. Mousie and Lousie did not say anything. They just let the others argue.

As eight o'clock approached, Mousie and Lousie quietly slipped away and out of sight. As the town clock struck eight tones, Mouse and Lousie returned to the present. They had been to the Wild West and had a feud with the future Billy the Kid. Mousie, in particular, felt lucky to be back home.

Mousie and Lousie:
Return to the Wild West

Having once visited the Wild West, Mousie and Lousie became more interested in some of its history. In particular, they were interested in the gunfight at the OK Corral. This gunfight took place October 26, 1881, at about three o'clock in the afternoon in Tombstone, Arizona. Actually, the gunfight occurred a few doors down from the OK Corral building. It began in a narrow lot where the opposing sides were in close range of each other and then spread out into the street. The gunfight lasted only about thirty seconds.

The opposing sides consisted of the outlaws and the lawmen. The outlaws were Billy Clairborn, Ike and Billy Clanton, and Tom and Frank McLaury. The lawmen were Marshal Virgil Earp and Deputies Morgan and Wyatt Earp and Doc Holliday. Of the outlaws, Billy Clanton, Tom and Frank McLaury were killed, while Ike Clanton and Billy

Clairborn ran from the fight. Of the lawmen, Virgil and Morgan Earp were wounded, while Wyatt Earp and Doc Holliday were not hurt. (Later on, Wyatt Earp would become marshal of Tombstone.)

What has remained a controversy is how the fight began. Who fired the first shot? One version has it that the outlaws had their hands up when the lawmen began to fire. A more believable version has it that the outlaws fired first. Forensic analysis (scientific methods of investigating crime) supports the view that none of the outlaws were shot with their hands up.

Mousie and Lousie wanted to go back in time to the day of the gunfight to witness just how it started. So they contacted Professor Ushgloshkiss Vernes and told him they would like to go back in time to 1881 in Tombstone, Arizona, to witness the start of the gunfight. The good professor told them that they could certainly set their pocket watch time machines for that location and date. He also told them not to bring their guns and holsters because, in spite of its bad reputation, residents of Tombstone were not allowed to carry firearms. The only exceptions were the marshal and his deputies.

So Mousie and Lousie put on their cowboy boots and cowboy hats, set the start time to 2:00 p.m., October 26, 1881, and return time 11:59 p.m. the same day. They set the location as OK Corral, Tombstone, Arizona. They checked that their time machine pocket watches were identically set, pressed the red buttons, and just like that they were back in Tombstone, Arizona. The first thing Mousie and Lousie did was check into the boarding house next to the OK Corral building. Then they took the alley going west past the OK Corral, past the narrow lot where the gunfight was to begin, and continued the short distance to Fremont Street.

There on Fremont Street was a saloon, which Mousie and Lousie decided to enter. So through the swinging gates of the saloon entrance came cowboys Mousie and Lousie. Some people were sitting at the tables having lunch. Others were playing poker for money. Others were having a drink at the bar. Lousie remembered from his previous journey back in time to the Wild West that it is not looked upon with favor to order chocolate milk at a bar, so instead he ordered whiskey, even though he had never drunk an alcoholic beverage before. Lousie drank it down in one gulp. Immediately his face turned red and his eyes looked like they were ready to pop out. But he said loudly so that everyone in the saloon could hear, "Ahhh, that was good whiskey! Bartender, I'll have another."

Meanwhile Mousie was not drinking. He was just sitting at the bar to give Lousie company. He started talking to Lousie about the day's events and, after a while, realized he was not getting any response. He looked over, and there was Lousie with his face flat on the counter. Mousie dragged Lousie over to one of the tables and ordered a pot of

coffee. After forcing Lousie to drink a couple of cups of black coffee, he started to get some response. At first Lousie did not know where he was or how he got there, but slowly his memory began to return.

Mousie was in a predicament. It was ten minutes to three o'clock. He could leave Lousie in the saloon and go watch the beginning of the gunfight, or he could get Lousie to bed at the boarding house and most likely miss the gunfight. In the end, his loyalty to Lousie won out, and he decided to take the quickest path with Lousie to the boarding house.

As it turned out, the quickest path to the boarding house went by the rear entrance to the OK Corral and the narrow lot where the gunfight began. Now that previously empty lot was no longer empty. Along one side were the lawmen. Along the opposite side were the outlaws. There was a heated exchange of words between the two sides. The atmosphere was like a stick of dynamite ready to explode.

Mousie and Lousie had no choice but to walk between these two sides in order to get to the boarding house. Mousie was just hoping that the gunfight would not start while they were caught in the middle. Mousie's pocket watch showed that it was almost three o'clock.

Lousie was unsteady on his feet and being supported by Mousie. In his unsteady state, Louise accidentally kicked up a large rock with his cowboy boot. The rock landed, making a cracking sound similar to a gunshot. The lawmen thought the outlaws had just fired a shot at them while the outlaws thought they were just fired upon by the lawmen. Then both sides started shooting at each other simultaneously. Mousie and Lousie, caught in the middle, quickly hit the ground and covered their heads with their hands. The gunshots went a long way toward sobering up Lousie.

The shooting quickly spread from the narrow lot out into Fremont Street. It all lasted for thirty seconds and then it was over. Mousie and Lousie, relieved and unhurt, got up and looked around. What they saw was as described in the history books. Nothing else in the details of the gunfight appeared to have changed. As Doc Holliday attended to the two wounded Earp brothers, Wyatt Earp came over to Mousie and Lousie and said, "You must be strangers to Tombstone. I have not seen either of you in this territory before." Then he asked, "Where are you from?" Lousie was about to answer, but Mousie, afraid that he might mention the pocket watch time machines, cut him off and answered instead. "We are just passing through on our way to New Mexico."

"In that case," said Wyatt Earp, "I'd advise you to stay clear of Fort Sumner. There is a dangerous outlaw out there who they call Billy the Kid. You don't want to meet up with him. He would eat you alive." Mousie thanked Wyatt for the advice. He and Lousie then left for the boarding house.

When they got there, they both went upstairs and right to bed. Being caught in the middle of a gunfight was enough excitement for a day. When they woke up the next morning, they were back home in their own beds.

So Mousie and Lousie settled the question of how the gunfight at the OK Corral began, but in doing so, they changed that part of history such that the gunfight started simultaneously from both sides, instigated by an accidentally kicked up rock that sounded like a gunshot when it landed.

Mousie and Lousie Visit Mars

As time went on, Mousie and Lousie again became interested in space. They had already gone to the moon. The next logical step would be to visit the planet Mars, one position farther from the sun than the Earth.

So Mousie and Lousie paid a visit to the good Professor Ushglosh-kiss Vernes and told him what they wanted to do. Professor Vernes said, "Yes, a trip to the planet Mars would be possible." But he would have to modify the rocket ship they took to the moon because building a new rocket ship from scratch would be too expensive.

The two mice agreed that was a logical choice, and so the good professor went about modifying the rocket ship they had taken to the moon, turning it into a rocket ship to go to Mars. One of the big improvements was the addition of a more powerful engine that was expected to cut the travel time from Earth to Mars down from eight months to one month.

While the inside of the rocket ship looked very much the same, Professor Vernes completely reprogrammed it so that the rocket ship would automatically follow a trajectory to Mars. Another change, this one to the interior, was the addition of an exercise room so Mousie and Lousie could remain in good shape during the weightlessness of outer space.

Finally the big day arrived when Mousie and Lousie would take off for Mars. The rocket ship went through its final count down and then they were off. Looking out the back window, Mousie and Lousie saw Earth slowly become smaller. Now they knew they were in deep space. On the instrument panel one thing that Mousie quickly noticed was the red button with the writing "You may or may not want to press this red button." Remembering from the moon trip that pressing the red button played a recording of Professor Ushgloshkiss Vernes singing opera with the worst possible voice, Mousie quickly covered up the red button with duct tape and that was that.

Mousie and Lousie brought games to play and books to read for the long journey, so time went rather fast. Sooner than they expected, the warning over the loudspeaker said, "Prepare for landing" as the rocket ship began to slow down in preparation for landing on Mars. Not long afterwards, they reached the surface of Mars. Mousie and Lousie put on their space suits along with oxygen tanks, so they could breathe, and walkie-talkie radios, so they could communicate. Then they left the rocket ship and took their first steps on Mars.

The surface consisted of red sand and a few rocks. The ground was mostly flat with indented craters here and there. There were two shiny objects in the distance. Mousie and Lousie decided to investigate what they were. When they were closer they realized the two objects were Spirit and Opportunity, each a six-wheeled solar-powered robot. These were the Mars exploration rovers (because they could move) designed in the United States to slowly travel over Mars and take pictures of what they see. The pictures could be of the landscape or close up examination of the soil. Spirit and Opportunity each had nine cameras. As Mousie and Lousie moved around the robots, more and more of the cameras focused on them. Soon all cameras were focused on Mousie and Lousie and taking pictures of them.

This gave the two mice an idea. Why not have a contest as to who can make the funniest face for the cameras. So Mousie and Lousie set about making all kinds of silly faces while the cameras on Spirit and Opportunity clicked away. It was just too bad there was no instant playback. They would have to wait until they returned to Earth to see how the pictures came out. But in any case, it was lots of fun.

Once finishing their photo shoot, Mousie and Lousie spent some time just admiring the view of space from Mars. Then they set about collecting samples of Martian soil and rocks of different shapes and sizes. When they were done with their collection, they returned to their rocket ship. After checking that everything was in order, they took off for the one month journey back to earth.

Meanwhile on Earth, their pictures were creating quite a stir. The pictures first arrived at NASA, the government agency responsible for space exploration, and from there, they were delivered to the newspapers and broadcast news stations. No one knew quite what to make of

these space mice and their silly expressions, so broadcast news looked for experts on space mice. Finding none, one station brought in what they thought was the closest thing—an exterminator. The exterminator said that what they were seeing was just the tip of the iceberg. If you see one space mouse, that means there are a thousand more that you don't see. And if you see two space mice, that means there are a million more that you don't see. Other stations copied this logic, so the official estimate of the number of space mice on Mars jumped from two mice to one million.

To explain the strange expressions of these space mice, another station brought in an expert on ancient civilizations. He said warriors in ancient civilizations used special facial expressions to get them pumped up and ready for battle. This expert said, "What we see here is an army of one million space mice getting prepared for battle with the maker of Spirit and Opportunity, namely the United States." This line of reasoning caught on, so now there were newspapers with headlines like ARMY OF ONE MILLION SPACE MICE FROM MARS READY TO ATTACK THE UNITED STATES.

This caused a great deal of panic, as people began to load up on food supplies and other necessities. They bought extra locks and bolts for their doors and windows. The army, navy, and air force were put on twenty-four-hour alert.

Professor Ushgloshkiss Vernes saw these headlines and listened to the reports on the news programs and quickly realized things were getting out of hand. He drove to Washington, DC, and arranged a meeting with NASA officials. He explained that Mousie and Lousie were just two fun-loving mice. There were not one million space mice on Mars ready to attack the United States. Besides, from the photographs, it was obvious they were seeing who could make the silliest face for the cameras. When asked how Mousie and Lousie got to Mars, Professor Vernes replied that they did it in a rocket ship that he built. The NASA officials were very impressed by the professor's expertise. In fact, they offered to hire him on the spot, which the good professor refused. He liked working with the intelligent mice from Mouseville.

Nevertheless, Mousie and Lousie had broken the law by interfering with a government mission and government property, but considering they meant no harm, the fine was reduced to one hundred dollars for each mouse, which Professor Vernes gladly paid.

So by the time Mousie and Lousie arrived back in Mouseville, one month after leaving Mars, things had gone back to normal. People were not stocking up on food items anymore, and the army, navy, and air force had cancelled their twenty-four-hour alert. Professor Vernes filled Mousie and Lousie in on the commotion they had caused. But Mousie and Lousie still wanted to see the silly pictures taken of them by Spirit and Opportunity. After carefully examining the pictures, and with Professor Ushgloshkiss Vernes as judge, the contest of who could make the funniest face for the cameras was declared a draw.

And, by the way, the Smithsonian paid the two mice two hundred dollars for the soil samples and rocks they had collected on Mars. This they used to pay back the good professor.

How Tiger Got His Stripes

Mousie and Lousie, Topsie and Wopsie were sitting on their porch one evening discussing folktales. Topsie said, "Here is a Vietnamese folktale about how Tiger got his stripes." Topsie went on and told the following folktale:

Long ago, Tiger had a beautiful golden coat without any stripes. One day, Tiger saw an ox plowing a field for a little animal. The next day, Tiger asked the ox, "Why work for this little animal? Surely you are much stronger." The ox replied, "That little animal is man, and he does not need strength because he has wisdom." Tiger thought about it and decided he wanted wisdom also. So

Tiger approached the little man while he was tending his goats and said, "Man, give me your wisdom or I will eat you." The man was frightened, but then he thought a moment and said, "Tiger, I can give you my wisdom, but I left it at home. If you will be so kind as to let me tie you to that tree so that you won't eat any of my goats while I am gone, then I will go home and bring it to you." The tiger agreed, so the man tied the tiger tightly to the tree and left, taking with him his goats behind Tiger's back. Tiger waited and waited for the little man to return with his wisdom, but he never came back. Finally, Tiger realized he had been tricked. He struggled with all his mighty strength and finally broke through the ropes. Later that day, Tiger was thirsty and went to the lake for a drink of water. He saw his reflection in the water, and to his surprise, there now were black stripes where the tight ropes had burned his skin. And that is how Tiger got his stripes.

Wopsie said, "That's a good folktale. Now let's make up our own. In each case, the legend begins long, long ago, when Tiger had a golden coat without any black stripes. I'll go first."

So here is what Wopsie made up:

Tiger was out hunting when, all of a sudden, the sky opened up and it rained very hard along with thunder and lightning and wind. Tiger was on top of a hill, and other than shrubbery, the only

thing around was a single tree. The tree called to Tiger, "Come under my branches, and my leaves will protect you from the wind and the rain."

"What about the lightning?" asked Tiger. "Have you ever been struck by lightning?"

"Yes," said the tree.

Tiger was glad to hear that because lightning never strikes twice in the same place, right? So Tiger lay down underneath the tree. Almost as if by magic, the leaves of the tree did keep tiger dry and warm and kept out the wind. Tiger soon fell asleep. The next morning, the storm was gone, but overnight, the tree had been struck by lightning. When Tiger woke up, he had burns on his body from the lightning strike. The burns quickly healed, but in their place, they left black stripes. And that is how Tiger got his stripes.

Mousie went next. So here is the folk tale that Mousie made up about how Tiger got his stripes:

Long, long ago when tigers had golden coats, they lived in small houses called huts. Tiger was painting his hut. Last but not least was the floor. Tiger wanted to paint a pattern on the floor, but he was getting tired of painting and decided to make the pattern as simple as possible. The pattern he chose was black stripes. When Tiger was just about finished painting the floor, he realized he had painted himself into a corner. The entrance was at the opposite end of the hut. Now Tiger could either wait for the paint to dry or he could walk over the wet paint to get to the entrance. Tiger was impatient and decided not to wait. But the wet paint was slippery. Tiger lost traction on all four legs and landed flat on his belly. Then he slipped again and landed flat on his back. But at least now he was at the entrance to the hut and could go out and do some hunting. Later, in the evening, Tiger was thirsty and went to the lake for a drink of water. In his reflection he saw the black stripes on his body. But by now, the paint was dry and would not come off. Many of the forest animals tried to help Tiger scrub off the paint, but it still would not come off. And that is how Tiger got his stripes.

Finally, it was Lousie's turn to make up a folktale. This is Lousie's version of how Tiger got his stripes:

There was a young tiger that had a habit of lying to his fellow tigers. The older tigers wanted to break him from this habit, so they consulted the wise old owl. The owl gave them a magic potion to add to the young tiger's drinking water. Every time the young tiger told a lie, a black stripe would appear on his coat. The length of the stripe would depend on the significance of the lie. The young tiger was afterwards told about the magic potion. Tiger noticed his beautiful golden coat filling up

with black stripes. He now tried very hard to stop
lying. Finally he stopped, but by then, he had a full
set of stripes. And that is how Tiger got his stripes.

So Topsie told a real folktale and Mousie, Lousie, and Wopsie each
made up a folktale about how Tiger got his stripes. Now how do *you*
think Tiger got his stripes?

Professor Vernes Invents Antigravity

One day, Mousie and Lousie paid a visit to Professor Ushgloshkiss Vernes to see what he was up to. Professor Vernes invited them into his laboratory to show them his latest invention—antigravity. For example, he painted the material on an ordinary rubber ball, and it rose up like a helium-filled balloon until it reached the ceiling. Mousie said, "That's great. Now you can make vehicles that fly through the air like airplanes." Professor Vernes replied that there was enough air traffic already without antigravity. He wanted a more exotic use of his invention. Mousie asked what he had in mind, and the professor replied, "Perhaps a pair of shoes that walk by themselves or run by themselves or dance by themselves or perhaps do all three. Lousie replied that that seemed a little farfetched. "Is that so," answered the good professor. "Then come with me."

They went into another room in the laboratory, and Professor Vernes showed them an ordinary looking pair of shoes and a remote control box. He placed the shoes on the floor and turned a control knob. Immediately, the shoes started walking by themselves. He turned up the control knob, and the shoes began trotting. He turned it up further, and the shoes began running until they crashed into the wall. "Obviously it still needs a little work," replied the professor.

Then Professor Vernes showed them another pair of shoes with a similar control box. "These shoes can dance," said the good professor. "First, let's do the fox-trot," said the professor as he turned a control knob. Mousie and Lousie could almost see a dancer wearing the shoes as they went through the steps. "Obviously there are many more dance steps I can program them to do," said the professor. "An amateur dancer can look like a professional wearing a pair of shoes like these. Similarly, an amateur runner can look like a professional athlete."

Mousie and Lousie were very impressed. Mousie asked, "So what is your next step going to be?" Professor Vernes replied that he planned to combine all functions under one remote control box. He would leave out walking and trotting because most people can do that. He would include running and a wide selection of dance steps.

Mousie asked Professor Vernes if he could use the shoes for the upcoming ten-mile run for competitors from the color counties. Every year, the best runners from each color county apply to run for their county. Then there is a drawing, and two runners are selected from each county. This year Mousie was selected as one of the two runners from their county, Orange County. Mousie would be the only mouse in the race. (The rest would be people.) It is a fun race. There is no money for the winner, just a gold-plated trophy. Now, Mousie is a good runner, but there are some better ones among the color counties. Mousie wanted to see if the shoes could actually win the race for him, and as it turns out, Professor Vernes was just as curious. So the good professor promised Mousie the shoes would be ready by the time of the race.

The racetrack was an oval of length half a mile for one complete circuit, so the winner would be the first runner to complete twenty circuits or twenty laps. Then the winner runs one more circuit, called the victory lap, to give the audience an opportunity to cheer for him or her. At the end of the victory lap, the winner stops at the mayor's booth for the presentation of the trophy and a short speech.

As promised, Professor Ushgloshkiss Vernes had the shoes ready by the time of the race. Professor Vernes was to work the control box that wirelessly controlled running or dancing. Also built into it was a two-way wireless link to allow the runner and person with the control box to communicate back and forth if need be.

On the day of the race, the fans filled the stadium to capacity. Lousie, Topsie, and Wopsie took their seats next to the good professor. Everyone was ready to have a good time. The race was to begin promptly at 7:00 p.m. The racers took their positions. All racers were wearing light shoes except Mousie. Each one of the racers was wondering how Mousie planned to do well with such heavy shoes. Then promptly at seven, the bell sounded, indicating the start of the race. All racers took off except Mousie, who was dancing the cha-cha. After a few seconds the good professor realized his mistake and pressed the correct button. Then Mousie too was off, but he had a lot of ground to make up.

Mousie, however, was running very fast in his remote-controlled shoes, and on each lap, he gained a little more ground. Finally, on the

fifteenth lap, he caught up with and then passed the leader. He increased his lead on each of the remaining laps. So Mousie was the first runner to complete twenty laps and, thereby, won the race. Not only did he win the race, he won by a landslide.

Now it was time for the victory lap. Once more Mousie circled the racetrack while the crowd stood up and cheered. The next step was to stop at the mayor's booth to pick up the trophy. But for some reason, the shoes would not stop. Mousie was starting a second victory lap. The crowd still cheered though not as much. The fans looked confused. So did the mayor, and so did Mousie. Mousie asked Professor Vernes over the two-way wireless link what was wrong. The good professor replied, "Mousie, I can't find the stop button." Mousie was shocked. How could Professor Ushgloshkiss Vernes forget to put a stop button on the control panel?

Mousie was now on his third victory lap. The mayor was leaving with an angry look on his face, and the stadium was beginning to empty out. By the fourth victory lap, the only ones still in the stadium were the professor, Lousie, Topsie, and Wopsie, and of course, Mousie.

Mousie asked the professor if he was making any progress finding the stop button. Professor Ushgloshkiss Vernes replied with a no, that he probably mislabeled the stop button as one of the dance routines. He would have to try out each of the dance routine buttons until he found which one was mislabeled and was the actual stop button. Either that or he just forgot to put in a stop button. This was a characteristic of Professor Ushgloshkiss Vernes. He was a genius who could come up with the most complicated inventions, but then he could forget the simplest things.

So Professor Vernes started going through the dance routines one by one, hoping one of them was the actual stop button. So one after another, Mousie danced the mambo, cha-cha, tango, fox-trot, merengue, rumba, salsa, samba, waltz, swing, disco, the hustle, Charleston, the jitterbug, and a few other dances.

It was getting late, and Mousie was very tired of running and dancing. The good professor told him, "I'm sorry, Mousie, but it seems I forgot to put in a stop button." Mousie replied, "Professor, I'm just too tired to dance or run anymore. If you can't find the stop button or if there is none, then there is no choice except to destroy the control panel."

The good professor finally agreed, so he asked Lousie, Topsie, and Wopsie to find a big rock so he could destroy the control panel. Soon the three mice returned with a large rock. Professor Vernes was very reluctant to destroy his invention, but he saw no other choice. He put the control panel on the ground face down and asked the three mice to smash it. It took all three of them to lift this large rock, and they were about to let go and drop it on the control panel when the good professor yelled out, "Stop!" There on the back of the control panel, all by itself, was a single button labeled STOP. So there was a stop button after all, placed on the back of the control panel to make it easy to find. That's the first place Professor Ushgloshkiss Vernes should have looked.

So the professor picked up the control panel, pressed STOP, and for the first time in five hours and with a great feeling of relief, Mousie was finally able to stand still. A bit later, with all four mice in Professor Vernes's car, they stopped at an all-night cafe and bought Mousie his favorite ice cream. Mousie had probably done the equivalent of a marathon that evening. He was one very tired mouse, and you can be sure he slept very well for the remainder of that night.

Acknowledgements

I would like to thank Penny Levy for encouraging me to write down these stories, to Eliza Nelson, who at age nine, came up with the initial concept drawing of the intelligent mice, and to David Rodax, my Publication Cordinator at Page Publishing for his guidance.

Many thanks go to my sister Alice, who recruited her friend and colleague Ruth to do the illustrations, and for her tireless help in editing this book.

Last but not least, I would like to thank Ruth Flanigan, for her delightful and beautiful illustrations, and for bringing Mousie and Lousie to life.

About the Author

Michael Schildcrout was born and raised in the Bronx, New York. He attended Hunter College, uptown campus. From there he went to the University of Pittsburgh where he earned a Ph.D. Degree in physics. Dr. Schildcrout then joined the navy (as a civilian) where he worked in naval intelligence for 34 years before retiring. He now resides in Worcester, MA. While there, he joined a writer's group. The group leader encouraged him to write down the stories he used to tell his younger sister, Alice, when she was little. With the passage of time, some of the stories had to be updated, others are new, but they all retain the original set of characters.

About the Illustrator

Ruth Flanigan has always loved to read and draw. Through her childhood and teen years, she and her dad would often go out sketching for the afternoon, searching for the perfect landscape or farmhouse to draw. When her parents would take the family to the Rhode Island School of Design Museum, she noticed the RISD students w/ their paint boxes and sketch pads, and decided her future path. She graduated from RISD and became an illustrator of children's literature, educational materials, and magazines. She continues to enjoy her job making pictures, and lives in Massachusetts with her husband, daughter, and two cats.

CPSIA information can be obtained
at www.ICGtesting.com
Printed in the USA
BVOW05s0249140817
491995BV00017B/353/P